Zoom
to the
Moon

Written by Hatty Skinner

Collins

Look up in the dark.

You might see the moon.

We see it up high.

It lights up the night.

On the moon you can see the sun.

Wow!

This rocket got to the moon.

fin

A man was on the moon.

helmet

boots

11

The rocket shot back down.

The men got back too.

Look at the moon!

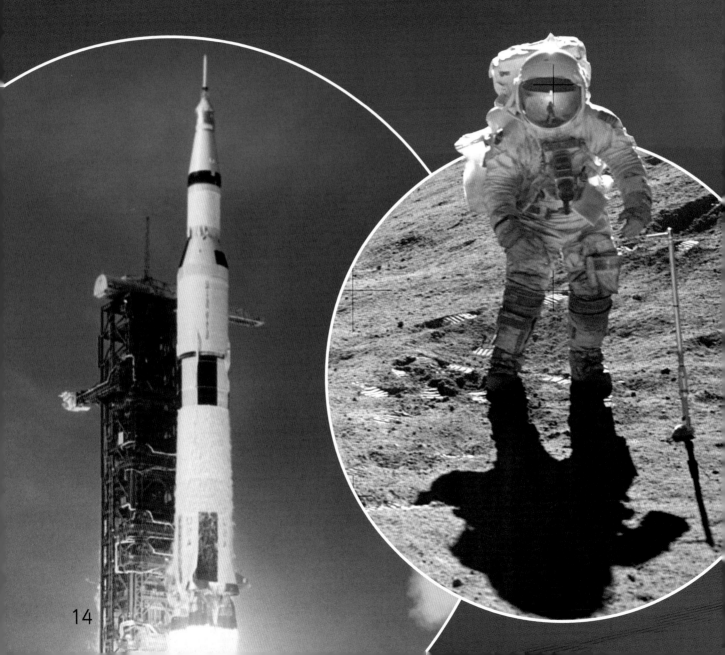

 After reading

Letters and Sounds: Phase 3

Word count: 58

Focus phonemes: /ee/ /igh/ /oo/ /oo/ /ow/ /ar/

Common exception words: you, the, we, was, to

Curriculum links: Understanding the world

Early learning goals: Reading: read and understand simple sentences; use phonic knowledge to decode regular words and read them aloud accurately; read some common irregular words.

Developing fluency

- Challenge your child to imagine they are a space expert and to read the text with enthusiasm. Remind them to read the labels, too, and to look out for an exclamation mark (which tells them to read a word with extra emphasis).

Phonic practice

- Remind your child that the letters "oo" together can make two different sounds. Can they sound out and blend these words correctly?

  l/oo/k   m/oo/n   b/oo/t/s   t/oo   z/oo/m

- On page 3, can your child find a word with an unusual spelling of an /oo/ sound? (Y/ou)

Extending vocabulary

- Reread pages 2–3 and discuss the meaning of **might**. Ask: What might you be able to do on the moon? (e.g. *I **might** be able to see Earth.*)